D0595018

Praying for Jennifer

Praying for Jennifer

John B. Cobb, Jr.

AN EXPLORATION OF
INTERCESSORY PRAYER
IN STORY FORM

THE UPPER ROOM
NASHVILLE, TENNESSEE

PRAYING FOR JENNIFER

COPYRIGHT ©*1985 by JOHN B. COBB, JR.*

All rights reserved.

Cover Design: Harriette Bateman
Book Design: John Robinson

First Printing: October, 1985 (5)
Library of Congress Catalog Card Number: 85-51240

ISBN 0-8358-0520-4

PRINTED IN THE UNITED STATES OF AMERICA

CONTENTS

THE PURPOSE of this book is to make sense of intercessory prayer. But instead of just laying out my own ideas, I thought it better to juxtapose several different ways of thinking about the subject. That suggested dialogue. And dialogue seemed to work best in the context of a story. Hence, this is theology in story form.

Although the primary topic is intercessory prayer, no discussion of that subject can avoid other questions. How are we to think of God and of God's acts in the world? What is the nature of divine power? Why is there so much perverse evil in the world? How do we sort out what God does and what we do? I hope that following the story along with the questions and arguments of the characters will help the reader come to clearer and more satisfying answers to questions such as these.

It is the policy of The Upper Room to use inclusive language in references to God. I support this policy. Nevertheless, I have requested that an exception be made in this instance. Much of the book consists of dialogue among persons who would be unlikely yet to speak in the new way about God, More important, the issue of language about God is raised in chapters 5 and 6, and this requires that conventional language be used in the dialogue prior to that point.

This book owes its existence to the stimulus and cooperation of a group of church persons who have met several times to encourage the Center for Process Studies to prepare materials for use in churches. David Polk, William Beardslee, and James Jacobson have been particularly helpful, while Judy Casanova has contributed extensively to both form and content. Don McIntyre, over a period of several years, prodded me to write on intercessory prayer. I kept saying maybe. Finally his persistence paid off.

The new program of the Center for Process Studies of which this book is an expression is called "Process and Faith." Readers interested in knowing more about this program should write to it, in care of the School of Theology at Claremont, Claremont, CA 91711.

John B. Cobb, Jr.

Praying for Jennifer

1 · JENNIFER'S FRIENDS

THE DOOR of Room 517 clicked softly behind them, and David and Janice stumbled into the antiseptic brightness of the hospital corridor. Behind the closed door lay their friend Jennifer, once bright and full of fun, but for the last three months, silent and unresponsive. Coma, the doctor called it, but for David and Janice it meant grief and guilt, bewilderment and almost unbearable loss.

Again and again, David relived the events of that May evening he could never escape. Time after time he saw himself and three friends leave the junior class party. He saw himself jump into the driver's seat, turn the key, and pull out of the parking lot. *Maybe I wasn't careful enough that night*, he thought once again, but he also remembered how happy they had been. Then he saw the lights of the other car and felt the sickening crunch of impact. *It really was the other driver's fault*, David kept telling himself, *even the police said so.*

Three of them—David, Janice, and Bill, Jennifer's date—had walked away with nothing worse than bad bruises. Even the car, after a thousand dollars and two weeks in the repair shop, looked the same as before. But Jennifer—caring, laughing, teasing Jennifer . . .

David hated coming to see her. And she certainly never knew whether or not he was there. It was worse when Jennifer's parents were there. They never blamed him directly—to be honest, they had tried to make him feel better—but seeing them only made him feel guiltier. Yet he couldn't stop coming—furtively, constantly, hopefully, desperately—each time searching for some change for the better, some little sign of the old Jennifer.

But today he felt real despair. Jennifer was having difficulty breathing. The nurse shook her head, and David knew that Jennifer was dying. If only . . .

Janice had been very close to Jennifer, much closer than David had been. She felt Jennifer's injuries in a keenly personal way. But just now she was even more concerned about David. *This could not have happened to a nicer guy*, she thought. There were plenty of carousers and wild drivers in the class, but David was not one of them. He was a sensible fellow, almost too sensible. That night he had let down a little, and she had liked it. She had even encouraged him. It was good to see David really enjoying himself instead of bearing all the problems of the world on his shoulders. And the wreck really hadn't been his fault. She had to get him away from the room. She guided him to the cafeteria on the ground floor.

"They're doing everything they can," she insisted.

"I know," David replied. "It just isn't going to be enough. The nurse said all we can do now is pray. That means it's hopeless."

"But maybe it's not," Janice blurted out, hardly believing what she was saying but desperate to penetrate his quiet despair. "Maybe prayer would help."

David said nothing for a long time, and in the silence Janice began to panic. *Now I've really upset him*, she accused herself. *Who am I to recommend prayer, anyway? I've never prayed seriously in my life. David's the one who grew up in church—and knowing me has made him less active in church, not more.* But she had heard of miraculous cures and had even watched television programs occasionally that featured spiritual healing. *Maybe we could contact one of those healers*, she thought. *We would at least be doing something.*

David recalled all the times in the past three months he had thought of Jennifer and had silently cried out, *Oh, God, don't let her die. Please, God, don't let her die.*

But God was, he reflected bitterly. *God was letting Jennifer die.* Then he remembered something about prayer groups; he had heard about how several people really praying together for someone sometimes made a remarkable difference. Finally, with the calmness of exhausted grief, David asked gently, "Janice, would you pray with me?"

Relieved and pleased and scared, Janice managed a "Sure," but she was far from sure. Tears welled up from her tangled emotions, and it was David who now comforted Janice as they abandoned their half-eaten hamburgers and stumbled outside.

As David drove her home—oh, so carefully— they made plans. David would invite Bill to join them, and Janice would invite Sharon, Jennifer's best friend. They would meet in Janice's living room, since her parents were away for a few days, and they could talk without anyone interrupting or overhearing. They wouldn't tell anyone else what they were doing.

Three very nervous teenagers arrived promptly at 7:30 at Janice's house the next evening. The conversation bumped from summer vacation to the new school year to who was dating whom. Finally, Sharon looked directly at Janice. "I thought we came here tonight because of Jennifer," she stated boldly. Immediately, the restless chatter ceased.

David saw Janice blanch; then he swallowed hard and took over. "Yes," he said, more firmly than he felt, "Jennifer is dying. The nurse said there was nothing anyone could do except pray. And Janice and I decided that we should try. Thanks for coming." It was the hardest speech he had ever made, but he was relieved to have begun, and he knew he had said what needed saying.

Bill was the first to respond. "I know, David.

You told me that yesterday. And I couldn't refuse to come. There's nothing I wouldn't do to bring Jennifer back. But you know I don't know anything about prayer. I don't think I even believe in God. I would feel silly just saying things to empty space."

Sharon was the most relaxed of the four. "Jennifer used to pray a lot, and once or twice we prayed together. I don't mind praying at all. I don't know who or what God is, but praying feels OK to me. When you want something, you've got to ask for it, and when there's no human being to ask, you've still got to ask. You shouldn't worry about what you believe, Bill. Just ask."

They all felt better after that, partly because Sharon seemed ready to take the lead. It was just a matter, then, of deciding what to ask for and how to ask. But that was settled, too, when they said together, "Dear God, don't let Jennifer die!" Saying it out loud, and saying it together, released something in them. They prayed again and again, sometimes crying, sometimes shouting, sometimes whispering. Sometimes they sounded demanding or angry. Sometimes they were beseeching and abject. Months of accumulated feeling came out. After a half-hour they were hugging each other, feeling lighter than they had felt since May. None of them dared to say it, but they had a sense that Jennifer was better.

Even so, David and Janice were not prepared

for what they saw the next day at the hospital. Jennifer was better. She was still in the coma, but her breathing was smoother. Indeed, there was nothing wrong with her breathing. And there was something else they both felt, though neither dared to speak about it. Her face looked different. Maybe it was the color. But, indescribably, it looked more alive.

A now-smiling nurse agreed, "The doctors were wrong. Yesterday evening she turned some kind of corner. Sometimes it happens. We don't understand it; we just give thanks."

Janice and David nearly fell over themselves in their haste to phone Sharon and Bill, and the four could hardly wait to get together again that night. Sharon and Bill kept pressing the other two for details— "The nurse said yesterday evening? Really? At what time? What do you mean you didn't ask? Well, what did she look like?"

"You know, it could be coincidence," Bill ventured at last, but it was clear that not even he believed that it really was. They were all more than ready to pray again. "Shall we pray the same way?" asked Bill.

Janice suggested that they ask God to bring Jennifer out of her coma, and they agreed, even though they felt a little presumptuous asking for so much so fast. But Sharon again took charge. "Prayer shouldn't be just asking. We ought to say thanks, too." And so they did. They prayed together, very simply indeed, "We thank you, God!" Saying that together out loud brought them together, to depths of feeling not less than their cry to God the night before to save Jennifer from death.

Afterward they asked God to bring Jennifer out of her coma. The mood was more sober, but the longings expressed in their words were profound. And they had a kind of belief that what they were doing could really help Jennifer. Before they went home, they planned to meet again the following evening. In the meantime Sharon and Bill would visit Jennifer. They would not report to Janice and David until evening unless there was some urgent reason.

Janice and David looked forward to the evening with keen anticipation. Their families and friends noticed the difference in them. Of course they shared the good news about Jennifer's improvement, and that served to explain the teenagers' heightened spirits. Sharon, David, and Bill all arrived at the same time, fifteen minutes early, and Janice was ready for them.

"How was she?" David blurted out as they entered the room.

"She's still in a coma," Bill answered. His words were disappointing, but his expression was one of elation. "But she looked so much better, so much more alive than when I saw her last week. I could hardly believe the change. And the nurse said there had been a moment yesterday evening when she seemed almost to come out of it. I couldn't resist asking her what time that was. She said she didn't know exactly, but that it must have been around nine. You know, I'm going to pray tonight like crazy!"

They all joined him in that craziness, not just that night but again and again in the weeks that followed. Janice's parents had come home, so the group had to find other places to meet, none as satisfactory. But that did not seem to matter. School began, and all the activities that went with it kept them busy. They couldn't meet every day. Still, nothing was as important to any of them as their times of prayer together. And Jennifer continued to improve. Within a week she was definitely out of the coma. Gradually some of her faculties returned.

But she did not become her old self. Her memory was badly muddled, and her personality was noticeably different. The old radiance was gone. She was petulant and irritable. She could not concentrate. She seemed more like a spoiled child of ten than the bright and lively Jennifer they had known. And it gradually became clear that her progress had stopped. Apart from some difficulty in walking and in articulating what she wanted to say, her physical recovery was almost complete. She could go home, but it seemed she would never resume her schooling or be a normal companion of persons of her own age.

Her friends went to see her often, but the joy was gone. It wasn't fun to be with her. They went out of duty and out of hope. The hope dimmed. The visits became less frequent.

Janice and David and Sharon and Bill kept praying. They prayed fervently for Jennifer's complete recovery. They pleaded with God. They made great promises of what they would do if God would fully heal her. Sometimes they expressed their anger with God. Nothing seemed to make any difference. Had God played a trick on them, encouraging them and then stopping with results that were ambiguous indeed? Jennifer was an unhappy child in a young woman's body, a child without prospects of ever growing up. Was this better than the death that had once seemed so imminent?

"There's no point in going on with this any longer," Janice stated one day. "We're wasting our time."

"I guess you're right," Bill agreed reluctantly, "but, you know, I'll miss our times together. I know we'll still be friends and all, but it won't be the same. The praying brought us all so close."

"I'm praying for all sorts of things now," Sharon admitted, "and while I can't say I've gotten any dramatic results like we did with Jennifer, it's been good for me. I feel better in lots of ways."

"I really need this group," David confessed. "And I need the praying. It's very hard for me to cope with the reality that Jennifer will never be whole again. I know even less than before what prayer is or what it's all about. I'm really confused."

"Well," Janice conceded, "let's not quit yet.

Maybe we should talk with someone who's been praying longer and might know more. I'm not sure I know anybody like that, but there has to be someone who could help us."

David, who had started back to his church youth group that fall, suggested that they talk with his youth counselor. She was a mature woman, his mother's age, he thought, and he was impressed with the way she sometimes prayed with the group. They all agreed then, if Mrs. Johnson would see them, they would like to talk with her.

2 · MRS. JOHNSON

MRS. JOHNSON reflected on her phone call from David. *"If* she would see them?" she thought. She was so pleased that they would come, she was downright nervous about the encounter. She had met Jennifer before the accident and had a deep concern for David, aware of how personally he was taking the accident. She knew Janice, a little, through David. Sharon and Bill she had not met. She knew that David had been seeing a lot of a few friends who were all concerned about Jennifer, but until he told her, she did not know that they had been praying. And indeed David had not said much about that when he called her. He had just said that they had prayed for Jennifer sometimes and that they were confused about prayer.

Mrs. Johnson was good with young people, and they were soon at ease in her living room, nibbling light refreshments and talking about Jennifer. Mrs. Johnson let them know how much she respected their sticking by Jennifer and one another through those difficult months. She said it was great that they had been praying for Jennifer, and she was sure that had helped. But she was not prepared for the full story that her warmth and understanding elicited.

Bill talked the most. "Jennifer was my girl friend. Mrs. Johnson, she was terrific. I can't tell you how much I miss her. I haven't dated anybody since the accident. Somehow I just couldn't, with her lying there not being able to know anything or have any fun at all. I have to be honest with you. I've never had any interest in religion at all, but I really liked Jennifer. I can't think of anything else except this awful accident that would have gotten me to pray. But I really did—we all did—and as we prayed, at least at first, she started to get better. Everybody expected her to die—all the doctors and nurses had given up—she wasn't even able to breathe by herself. And the very first time we prayed, she turned a corner. Soon they took her off the respirator. And as we prayed, she began to get better in other ways, too. So we were all con-vinced that God had heard us and answered our prayers. But now it's all stopped—I mean we're still praying but Jennifer isn't getting any bet-ter—and she still has a long way to go. So now I don't know what to think. Why would God answer our prayers for awhile and then quit?"

Mrs. Johnson was astonished. She prayed reg-ularly, but she had never had such a dramatic experience as had these young people in the answer to their prayer. Of course, she had heard many such stories, and she believed them. She believed now what Bill told her. There was no doubting the sincerity of the four young people. God had answered their prayers! Why, indeed, had God stopped halfway?

She had heard various answers to this question. Some said it was to test our faith. If prayer were always answered straightforwardly, where would the faith be? We are called to pray without ceasing. The real test would be whether these youths continued to pray when there was no apparent answer or when the answer was no!

But somehow that did not seem the right thing to say. God couldn't be playing that kind of game with these fine young people, even if it seemed that way to them. They had persisted long after the improvement stopped—longer than she would have persisted, she suspected. What did God want of them? And could God leave Jennifer in her pitiful condition just to teach a lesson to the ones who had been praying for her? No, that wouldn't do.

"God's ways are indeed mysterious," she said out loud. "I don't know any Christian who isn't puzzled. The puzzle is expressed all through the scriptures, too. Sometimes later, looking back, what happened makes sense. We can see that God did have a good reason. But it doesn't always work that way. Paul wrote that now we see in a mirror dimly (1 Cor. 13:12). He was sure that in the end all would become clear to us. To live in faith is to be confident of that."

David was far from satisfied. "But why should we believe that it will all make sense in the end when it makes so little sense now? Isn't it just as likely that what we call faith will turn out to be wishful thinking?"

Mrs. Johnson had asked herself that same question a hundred times. One of her children had died in infancy. Another had gotten in trouble with drugs, and even now she could have no confidence that he was straightening out. Why did all that happen? She was reconciled to not understanding, but she knew that with young people it was not enough just to say they must believe. David's question was honest. God could not be angry with honest questioners. She was sure of that.

"That's a tough question," she answered. "I've asked it, too, many times, because I've had some real disappointments in life. But I think there are reasons to believe in God. Your own experience with prayer is one. And the stories in the Bible provide other reasons. For me, the most important is that of the crucifixion and resurrection of Jesus. It's true that Jesus is the only one who has risen. But he rose to assure us all that in our turn we would rise, too. Of course, the resurrection is a great mystery. But it does seem to tell us that even the worst events don't overcome the assurance that everything will be all right in the end.

"I have the sense that God reveals his power enough to let us know that we can trust him. There must be some reason that he doesn't just set aside all evil and bring about the final good right away. He seems to have some plan for history. Again, he gives us glimpses, but he wants us to trust him for the rest."

"That helps," conceded Janice, "but I'm still awfully confused. If God has a plan, did it include Jennifer's recovering in part and only in part? I don't understand that plan. As you say, maybe it will make sense to us someday, but if that was God's plan, does that mean our praying had nothing to do with it? Was it just a coincidence after all? Will God do what he wants to do regardless of what we do?"

"You do ask mighty good questions," answered Mrs. Johnson. "I'm sure it wasn't just a coincidence. And I'm sure that your praying was as important a part of God's plan as what happened to Jennifer. God put the idea of praying for her into your head, Janice. I'm sure of that. God guided all of you in your praying. And God used that in healing Jennifer. But, of course, God could have helped her without any of that. God can do whatever he wants.

"In this case I think I can see some of God's reasons for having healed Jennifer through your prayers. It has been a rich experience for you four. I'm sure that God has a plan for each of you and that bringing you to think about him and to pray to him as you have is an important part of that plan. Maybe stopping the healing process at this point is a part of that plan, too. I don't know. I'm as confused as you are about that. For my part, I'm certainly going to start praying for Jennifer and for you, too. Maybe that's part of God's plan—to draw me in and help me grow, too. I suppose God could do it all in other ways, but *this* is the way he has chosen. We can't expect to completely understand that."

Sharon broke in. "Maybe you're right. I've certainly found that I've grown a lot spiritually in these months. God has become very real to me. I haven't joined a church or anything, but I have dropped in on worship services. In the past occasionally going to churches with friends meant nothing to me, but now I sense that something important is going on and that I want to be a part of it. God seems to be leading me into something. I'm praying for guidance, and although I don't get any great revelations, I have a general sense that doors are opening in some directions and closing in others. I think I can trust him even without understanding."

"Well, I can't," David interrupted. "Look, Sharon, I believe everything you're saying. In many ways our times of prayer together have been the richest experiences of my life. I'm sure I'll never be the same again. I feel a part of the church in ways I never did before.

"But when we talk this way, we are describing a world in which everything follows according to God's plan. I can't stand that. I just can't believe that that awful accident I would give anything to undo was part of God's plan. If Jennifer fully recovered, maybe I could believe that. But I can't believe an all-powerful God would crush

Jennifer just to help us grow spiritually. No! That is too awful. I would hate a human being who would do something like that. I can't love God if I have to believe that. It's even worse with God. God can accomplish his purposes any way he wants. What possible reason can there be for him to choose such a cruel way? No!" David's voice had grown shrill and he was almost sobbing. "That accident was evil. If God willed it, he just isn't God."

"You're right, David," Mrs. Johnson said tenderly. "Christians don't look for God in wars and accidents. We see God in peacemaking and healing. We don't understand the evil in the world. It doesn't make sense. Sometimes we blame it on the devil, sometimes on ourselves. Sometimes we think there's a place for accidents that are no one's fault but are no less evil. I think we have to leave it at that. Somehow that's all part of God's plan, too, but we can't understand why. We just can't say that God caused the accident in the same way that we talk of God's having given Janice the idea of your praying together. We know God in Jesus, and Jesus didn't cause meaningless suffering. He healed and helped. The rest we don't understand. We just have to accept things as they come. We have no choice. And it helps to believe that everything fits into a plan that will make sense to us in the end."

David was soothed by her love, and he became quiet and listened, although he was not satisfied with what he heard. It seemed that he should not talk about evil as being part of God's plan. He should always talk about the good. But what if God willed the evil, too? *If that is true,* David thought, *I can never really love or trust him.* But for now he would listen. Mrs. Johnson was a great woman—and a great Christian. He was glad they had come.

"There's something else that bothers me about all this," said Bill. "I can see that getting us to pray might be part of God's plan. It has certainly had an effect on me. I don't know where I'll come out of all this, but I'll certainly be different and, I think, better. But it seems to me that what was good about our praying was that we weren't praying for ourselves. We were praying for Jennifer. Of course, we were hurting a lot, and maybe if we had prayed for God to make us hurt less, that would have helped. But right now that doesn't seem good to me. The hurting seemed right then, and it seems right now. I still hurt for Jennifer. I don't want God to take that away from me. And I don't want to pray for my own spiritual growth. If I've grown, it is because I prayed for Jennifer.

"But now it seems as though I was tricked some way. God was going to do for Jennifer whatever fitted his plan. It was for my sake that I was drawn into taking part. That doesn't feel right to me. It didn't seem that way when our prayers were most real. It seemed that what happened to us was incidental."

"I'm sure you're right about that, Bill, even if

I can't explain it very well." Mrs. Johnson knew she was in over her head. But she had to share herself, even if she couldn't solve the puzzles. These young people had come to a depth of spiritual insight she had rarely met, and she knew that she would need to send them to someone else, someone who had studied the Bible more and knew more about theology. For now, all she could do was to encourage them and share her own faith as honestly as she could.

"I'm sure that if you had just prayed for yourselves, God would have heard you. But I'm also sure that your deep love of Jennifer and your faithful praying for her touched God's heart in a special way. Somehow I don't think the same healing would have occurred without it. I wish I understood that. I don't. I've been helped often by Jesus' words when he said that in order to find our lives we have to lose them (Matt. 10:39). You forgot yourselves in your concern for Jennifer. That was important. Very important.

"I really appreciate your coming tonight and sharing with me. You've given me more than I've given you. I hope you'll come back. But I know when I've reached my limits. I've found it possible to live with my answers to these questions. And it hasn't been easy. When I give others my answers as I have tonight, I hear their inadequacy all the more clearly. You need to talk with someone else. I'm sure our pastor would be pleased to talk with you."

"I thought of going to him," David said, "but

he always seems so busy. And I don't think he likes young people very much. You make us feel at home. We can say to you whatever we really feel and think. I'm afraid we couldn't do that with Dr. Robinson."

"I can understand why you feel that way," Mrs. Johnson answered. "But I'm sure Dr. Robinson would really like to get to know you. He's very serious, you know, and he thinks that high school youths aren't interested in what he has to say. So he feels uncomfortable around you. He's told me that. You know that the discussions at our youth meetings don't stick to serious topics very long. Nothing like what happened here tonight has ever happened there. Dr. Robinson would love to talk with you about these questions. He would really be grateful for the chance.

"I'll tell you what. I'm as eager to hear his answers as I am for you to hear them. Would you let me set up a time and come with you? Maybe both you and he would feel more comfortable."

David agreed gratefully, and they set some dates to check out with Dr. Robinson. Then they decided to pray together. It felt right to include Mrs. Johnson in the prayer group. She didn't try to lead. She just shared in the style they had developed. With them she cried out in pain and hope that Jennifer might be restored to herself and to them. She had never been a part of such fervent prayer. She felt joy and pain together with them.

Finally, when they were through, she prayed, "I thank you for these young people. I'm sure you are leading them into new paths for your sake and theirs. They have already brought much to me. Be with them in their suffering and their hope. Hear their prayers for Jennifer. Give them the wisdom to understand as I have never understood. And help them to accept your will even when they do not understand. Amen."

The four youths left with tears in their eyes. They were glad they would see Mrs. Johnson again.

DR. ROBINSON was excited about the prospects of an evening of serious theological discussion with Mrs. Johnson and her young friends. Indeed, he would have been delighted at the prospects of theological discussion with anyone! He had enjoyed theology in seminary, and he had done well. He had brought questions with him, and these had been changed by his study. He felt that the new questions had been answered—not completely—but enough so that he had something to offer to lay people who were theologically perplexed. He had been disappointed that people rarely put their questions to him in theological terms. He had started out preaching theologically, but over the years he had found that people responded better to more psychologically worded sermons. He had adjusted, but uncomfortably. *In the church we should be able to talk theologically*, he thought.

The stiffness with young people which David had noticed expressed this disappointment. Dr. Robinson had experienced doubts as an adolescent, and he had thought that he would be able to help young people in his churches with theirs. But they didn't come to him with their doubts. He saw that in order to win their confidence he would have to be with them in all sorts of roles, and he didn't have the temperament for that. He admitted that he probably had neither the interest nor the patience. It was easier to deal with other adults, especially with those already committed to the work of the church. They didn't raise theological questions very often, but at least they could talk about the church and about how to improve the programs. On that score they had done quite well.

But tonight there would be a chance to talk unapologetically about the problem of evil and intercessory prayer. At least that's what Mrs. Johnson had indicated over the phone. He bowed his head and asked that God would show him how to communicate to these youths, how to hear what they were saying, and how to reply in ways that would not seem pompous and authoritarian. He really wanted to help them, and Mrs. Johnson had assured him that they were bright and serious. Very bright and very serious, she had said.

Mrs. Johnson and the four young people arrived together. They had gone by her house and then come in her car. They clearly wanted her to take the lead. She wished it were not necessary, but she accepted her role. Once they had exchanged greetings and seated themselves, she began. "Dr. Robinson," she said, "you're in for a treat. The evening I spent with these four young people was the highlight of all my youth work—

and you know I enjoy it all. The tragic accident that nearly killed Jennifer Hodgson brought these friends of hers together in a new way. They were led to become a prayer group, even though that was a new venture for all of them. At first their prayers were answered in a really marvelous way. You know the doctors did think that she was going to die. And it was just when they began to pray for her that she began to recover. They were excited, and they prayed all the more fervently. And then her recovery stopped halfway. Physically she's doing fairly well, but mentally she seems to have lost a great deal. The doctors give no hope for her ever being normal again. And certainly she's not improving now.

"That has been heartbreaking for a lot of people, but especially for these friends who have invested so much of themselves in her recovery. They don't understand what has happened. And when I tried to explain, I only made matters worse."

"That's not true," Janice broke in. "It was a wonderful evening for us, too. You helped us think way past anywhere we had been before. Mrs. Johnson is great, Dr. Robinson, but we did leave with new questions."

"I know Mrs. Johnson is great," replied Dr. Robinson sincerely. "And I don't know whether I can help in any way she couldn't. But I surely appreciate your giving me the chance. Can you tell me the kinds of questions you ended up with that night?"

David introduced his topic first. "Mrs. Johnson helped us to see that God has a plan and that Jennifer's partial healing and our praying were all part of that plan. She said that we could get glimpses of the plan now but much of it we couldn't understand until later. That made sense, even though I don't like to think part of God's plan is letting Jennifer stay where she is now. But then I realized that if everything happens according to God's plan, then even the accident was God's plan. I couldn't accept that. Every time I think of it that way, I just get angry with God. And when I think of God the way I learned in Sunday school, I just can't believe that God willed to hurt Jennifer that way. I liked Mrs. Johnson's way of responding to me, but I wasn't satisfied. She wasn't either. That's why she suggested that we come to you."

Dr. Robinson relaxed more and more. David was bright and serious, very bright and very serious. And the problem of evil was one Dr. Robinson had thought about often. Indeed, his professor at seminary had helped him with similar questions. It was time to pass on what he had learned, what had helped him to make sense of a world of cruelty and suffering that bore little relation to what people deserved.

"That's a very old question, David, and a very important one. Even in the Bible there's no single answer. The whole Book of Job wrestles with that question, and it comes up in lots of other places, too. I can't tell you *the* Christian answer. I suppose each Christian has to work it out individually. But I can share the answer that has helped me the most.

"The problem has to do with human freedom. Let's suppose that God had a plan for the world and just carried through that plan. We wouldn't have any freedom. We would just be puppets. Maybe everything would go smoothly, and we would all be happy. But what would be the point? Why bother with a creation like that?

"What God wanted was free creatures who could freely obey his will. The chosen obedience of a free agent is infinitely more valuable than the controlled movements of the arms and legs of a puppet. I think everyone agrees to that. But if there was to be free obedience, there had to be the real possibility of free disobedience. That meant that God had to keep his hands off his creatures, so to speak. God had to limit the exercise of his own power. Of course, God *could* stop us when we go wrong, but he doesn't. Not because he likes to see us suffer and make others suffer, but because he knows that to interfere would be to destroy our freedom which is his greatest creation."

"That makes a lot of sense, Dr. Robinson," David said gratefully. "I'll have to think about it. I guess that means that I and that hit-and-run driver who struck my car used our freedom wrongly, and God did not stop us. Jennifer was the innocent victim of our sins. That's not comfortable; it leaves me feeling responsible. But it fits the way things really seem to be. And I would rather admit that I did wrong than to think that God did it to Jennifer."

Mrs. Johnson was intrigued, "I think I've thought God left a lot to us, too, but I also thought that God's plan must govern everything. Are you saying that there really isn't any plan? Does God just turn everything over to us and leave us alone? That sounds pretty bleak. What happens to the Christian experience of grace and to the idea of providence? I can see the advantage of thinking of God as leaving us free, but surely he hasn't just left us to stew in our own juices!"

"You're right, Mrs. Johnson!" Dr. Robinson agreed. "I didn't mean to say that God just created the world and then left it to run its own course. That doesn't fit with what the Bible teaches at all. God does a lot for us. The Bible is filled with examples of the things God has done for people. And I'm convinced that God is present now, working with us. But there's a big difference between helping or directing us and *determining* what we do. One way we are free creatures, and the other way we're not.

"When we look at nature, we see a world in which there is no freedom. There God's will reigns in the form of natural law. When you push a stone over the edge of a cliff, it falls.

Maybe, occasionally, for some very special reason, God changes that. I don't know. But with
human beings, everything is different. When we
are slapped on one cheek, we may respond
angrily and hit back, or we may turn the other
cheek. God never takes that freedom away from
us. He has told us that it is better to turn the
other cheek, and he has established the church
to keep that teaching alive. I think the Holy
Spirit reminds us of it when the time comes. But
we remain free to get angry and strike back, and
I'm afraid that's what most of us do."

"How does that fit with the idea of predestination?" Mrs. Johnson wanted to know. "Isn't that
biblical teaching?"

Dr. Robinson expected that one. "I think that
the references to predestination are fewer than
people usually think and that too much emphasis has been put on them. References to God's
hardening people's hearts don't fit with what
I've said either. I worry about that. But I'm not
sure that anyone could ever take a theological
position that would be consistent with everything in the scriptures. We have to realize that
they were written by human beings over a
period of more than a thousand years. However
inspired they are by God, they reflect human
ways of thinking, too.

"The much more basic ideas in scripture are
election and covenant. God calls us, calls us to
quite specific roles. He called Israel, and he
established a covenant with Israel. God is always

faithful to his call and promise. But that did not guarantee the faithfulness of Israel. The Jewish scriptures are remarkably frank and honest about how often Israel was disobedient. The idea of predestination accents the faithfulness of God in his election of us. I don't think we should use it to imply that we are no longer free or that how we exercise our freedom is unimportant."

Bill was growing impatient. "I'm not sure I know what you're talking about. It all sounds like something I might want to study someday. But we came to talk about prayer, and I'm even more confused about that. It sounds like you're saying that God wouldn't interfere with what was going on in Jennifer's body. In that case it was coincidence after all that she began to improve just when we began to pray."

"That's an awfully hard one for me," Dr. Robinson confessed. "Every Sunday morning I lead the congregation in intercessory prayers, and I wonder what that is really supposed to do. Some things I'm quite sure of, and that keeps me going. I'm sure we should be concerned about others, and I'm sure we should express our concerns about others and about ourselves before God. When we express our concerns before God and ask in Jesus' name, our concerns are themselves purified. We find we can't pray that those with whom we happen to be angry have a miserable time. We've learned that even in war we can't simply pray that our side will be victorious when we know what that means for others of God's children. And that carries over into our thinking and feeling the rest of the time. We look at the world more from God's perspective rather than from a narrow, selfish viewpoint. This works for me, at least partially. I've learned that when I am angry, I should always pray for the one with whom I am angry. I won't say that the anger disappears immediately. But I will say that it subsides and that I can usually avoid acting on it. We Americans ought to pray much more often for the people and rulers of the Soviet Union. If we did, we couldn't think and act the way we do now."

Bill was far from satisfied. Dr. Robinson made a lot of sense, but he didn't seem to come to the point. "But we weren't angry with Jennifer, Dr. Robinson. We wanted her healed before we prayed, and we wanted her healed after we prayed. I don't see that what you're talking about as intercessory prayer has much to do with what we've experienced."

Dr. Robinson knew that Bill was right. He knew that he wanted to talk about what he did understand and that he really didn't understand how intercessory prayers helped those who were being prayed for. "I hate to admit it, Bill, but you're right. I think that what I was saying would have some bearing on your experience but probably not much. You would have continued to visit Jennifer whether or not you prayed for her, but I can't help thinking that both the frequency of your visits and the quality of what you communicated to her, the patience with which you dealt with her even when she did not respond as you hoped, were influenced by the time you had spent praying for her. Still, that's not the point. You want to know whether your prayers helped Jennifer.

"It is ironic, isn't it? If we go with the idea that God is sovereign and controls everything, it doesn't seem to make much difference what we do. That might apply to all our acts, but it seems particularly true of intercessory prayer. But if we take the other tack, as I do, and say that God limits himself, that he leaves us a wide area of free choices, we are just as puzzled as to how one person's prayer could affect another person's body. And I'm afraid I've just gone along not expecting it.

"On the other hand, I've heard so many stories like yours that I've not remained satisfied with dismissing them all as coincidences. Indeed, I've had a few experiences myself that shook me loose from that skepticism. So I have tried to think about it.

"I'm afraid that I'll still come at it rather indirectly, Bill. Please be patient with me. It may be the fault of academic training. Ask a professor a simple question, and expect a fifty-minute lecture in reply!

"My thinking began with the question of how we are related to our own bodies. There was a time when Western thinkers taught that our minds and our bodies were so different that they could not really affect each other. Medical science for a long time tried to deal with the condition of the body without reference to the soul. But hardly anyone is satisfied with that now. Doctors know that bodily health is affected by emotions and attitudes. Since prayer affects our emotions and our attitudes, it can certainly affect our bodies.

"That helps me one step in understanding intercessory prayer, too. If my prayer affects the way I relate to my sick neighbor, that can have an effect on his or her feelings, too. If I radiate confidence in the healing power of God, my neighbor may become more confident, and that confidence may enable the healing work of God in the body to proceed.

"But, Bill, I know that still doesn't deal with your experience. Jennifer began recovering when you were a couple of miles away. In any case she was in a coma, and it is hard to see how your feelings and attitudes could affect her in that condition. Frankly, I don't think it was a coincidence, or not just a coincidence. But I can't bring myself to think that God suspended natural laws or violated human freedom. I'm really in a bind on this one."

Sharon perked up when Dr. Robinson spoke of the effect of emotions and attitudes on one's own body and of the difficulty of thinking of such effects on the body of a distant person lying in a coma. "I know of a man who holds workshops on the power of prayer. He actually has his groups perform experiments. I think they sometimes pray for plants, and that makes them grow faster. Do you think it would be worth talking with him, Dr. Robinson?"

"I've heard of him, too, Sharon. His name is Firestone. Most of what I've heard is positive. Some people think he's a crackpot, but I suspect we too quickly reject people who have something to say that doesn't fit with our prejudices. I have a hard time understanding how what goes on in my mind could have an effect on the cells in a plant, but for a long time people had difficulty in comprehending that their minds could have an effect on the cells in their own bodies. There's a lot we don't know. God has made this world more marvelously than we have yet imagined."

The young people were excited about the prospect. Mrs. Johnson knew Mr. Firestone slightly. She warned them that he might not want to visit with them informally as she and Dr. Robinson had done. After all, he made a living leading workshops. They were fairly expensive, but she had heard of one-day workshops for fifty dollars.

Sharon thought a moment. "We could all chip in and send one person. I vote for Janice. She's been quiet this evening, but I know she's taken everything in. And I've heard her in class giving reports. She's great. If she goes and tells us about it afterward, we'll all benefit."

David and Bill quickly agreed. Janice started to demur, but she was flattered, and she really wanted to go. Also, she knew that declining would just lead to the others working harder to persuade her. "Thanks," she said, "I'm really pleased. I promise I'll do my best to share with you."

"And I'll really appreciate it if you come back here for the report," Dr. Robinson added. "I want to make my contribution to the kitty, and I want to learn more about what Mr. Firestone has to say. One of these days maybe I'll take the time to go to one of his workshops myself. I've become convinced this evening that I don't understand much about intercessory prayer."

They all agreed to the plan. They had been a little disappointed that Dr. Robinson could not explain more of what they wanted to know, but they had begun to like him. They could sense that he really did want to communicate with them and that he took his share of the blame for his frequent failures with young people. And they appreciated his honesty and openness to learning. The ten dollars he took out of his wallet helped, too. Mrs. Johnson added ten dollars, and Janice said she could afford ten. That left just twenty dollars for the other three.

While this was going on, Dr. Robinson was studying the newspaper. He found a small ad on Mr. Firestone's workshops. "We're in luck. There's a workshop a week from Saturday in a church not far from here. The charge is fifty dollars including lunch and a book written by Mr. Firestone. Will that work for you, Janice?"

It would. So everything was set. "Could we meet here the next day? Sunday afternoon around three?" Dr. Robinson asked. Everyone agreed.

4 · MR. FIRESTONE

JANICE was a little nervous but excited when they met again. The workshop had suggested to her a quite different way of looking at things, a way that seemed to fit her experience and to be comfortable for her. "Thanks again for sending me," she began. "It was a rich day. I wish you could have been there. So much of what we learned we had to take on faith. In the full course people test it out for themselves. Mr. Firestone kept telling us this, and I don't think it was just a come-on to get more students. I'll do the best I can to give you the gist of what he said, especially as it has to do with intercessory prayer.

"The first thing Mr. Firestone did was to get us to talk about how we saw the world, what the most important things were to us. It took a lot of guidance from him before much came of this, but gradually we began to see that some of us thought of the world as being made up of separate, independent things—buildings, mountains, stars, and people. Others put emphasis on relationships. For them, things weren't important except as they were related to other things. People didn't seem to exist so independently. Families were important units.

"Mr. Firestone claimed that we were expressing two different world views. One of them, he said, was the modern, scientific world view. (It's not really very 'modern.' Mr. Firestone said the idea arose in the seventeenth century!) We could think of that as a world of atoms in motion. In that real world there were no sounds or colors. The atoms never changed. They just moved in relation to one another. Tables and dogs are just two configurations of the same sorts of atoms. He admitted that most people who thought of the world that way thought there was another world of the mind as well, but, as Dr. Robinson told us last time, they had trouble seeing how mind and matter could interact.

"Mr. Firestone went on to say that that world view has been crumbling for a long time now. Especially contemporary physics can't fit its findings into it. I don't understand anything about relativity and quantum and fields and Bell's theorem, so I just listed those and won't try to explain at all. Mr. Firestone admitted that he was confused by much of what was going on in physics, but he was convinced that it pointed to a world in which the things that make it up are very interconnected.

"His own field was biology. He doesn't claim to be a scientist, but he has kept up some with events in the field. He said he never did like the way that so many biologists talked about animals as if they were really like machines. The biologists seemed to think that the way to explain what animals did was to study their organs, cells and, finally, chemistry. He was glad that some of his teachers, one in particular, talked about that problem. He called it 'reductionism'—reducing biology to chemistry and chemistry to physics. Mr. Firestone agreed with the teacher who criticized reductionism. Biology should look for the explanation of animal behavior in the interaction of animals with their environment, not in dissection and analysis of the parts of the animals.

"Later on Mr. Firestone saw that the difference among his teachers was one of world view. Some of them accepted the older scientific world view; they were looking for the final explanation in terms of matter in motion. A few of them accepted relationships as fundamental. They thought animals could be understood only in their natural habitat. They had a kind of empathy for the animals they studied. And they thought that even when they studied cells, they needed to see the cells in context, as parts of the organs in which they were located.

"Mr. Firestone admitted that all that seemed a long way from the effectiveness of prayer. But he said that he had found over the years that people who lived according to the older scientific world view, without even recognizing that they did so, just would not believe what he was saying about prayer. Even when he demonstrated the truth of his claims by experiments, they assumed they were being tricked. So he decided he needed to set these world view questions before us.

"Since I was one of those who had put the emphasis on relations, I was glad to be on the 'right side,' so to speak. Actually most of the women were thinking relationally. Anyway he insisted that contemporary scientific evidence favors relational thinking in biology as it does in physics. He pointed to the new prominence of ecology as doing a lot to make this apparent. The ecologists have been pointing out all sorts of interconnections which had been neglected by the rest of us.

"Finally, he began to show the relevance of all this to our religious thinking, specifically to prayer. Like Dr. Robinson, he emphasized how intimately our bodies and our minds are related to each other. What we think and feel affects the behavior of our cells. He shared with us the results of experiments with cancer patients. These were really impressive. The healthy cells definitely do better when people imagine them doing better! Of course, the condition of our bodies has a great effect upon our moods and attitudes. He told us of how chemical treatment has cured some supposedly psychological problems. He didn't spend as much time on that side of the matter. He just wanted to assure us he believed it.

"The point at which he went beyond what you

told us, Dr. Robinson, is when he started talking about what he called 'psi effects.' They include mental telepathy, but they also include other things I had not heard of before. The general point is that everything is related to everything and there is no great difference between what we call mind and what we call matter. Our thoughts and feelings affect the cells in our own bodies, but they affect the cells in other bodies and even plants. Sharon had told us about praying for plants, and that was one of the things that Mr. Firestone said they experimented with in the full-length workshop.

Everyone plants two boxes of marigold seedlings and then brings them to the workshop. They mix them all up and take two boxes home without knowing who planted them. Then each day they pray over one of the boxes for ten minutes. They are also encouraged to pray against the plants in the other box—to curse them, so to speak. He has kept records for eight years now, and he shared his results with us. They are not consistent. Occasionally someone brings in the report that the prayers made no difference, or even that the plants that were cursed have done better than the ones that were prayed for. But in more than 90 percent of the cases, there is a discernible difference in favor of the ones that have been blessed. He also told us about a book written by the Reverend Franklin Loehr some years ago, *The Power of Prayer on Plants*. He encouraged us to read it. He had gotten some of his ideas from it. He said that if we did not believe this, we should try the experiment on our own. Well, I believed him.

"Of course, his main interest was not in making plants grow faster and healthier. He said that getting people to see the effects they can have on plants encouraged them to believe that their prayers for sick people can help the cells in their bodies, too. That's what he's most interested in. He recommends praying near the sick body, as the experimenters pray near the plants. He thinks that the laying of hands on the diseased part of the body often helps, but distance is not a major obstacle. If we concentrate on the person from a distance, the effects are similar. He read us stories of Jesus' healings to show the variety of the ways they took place.

"I had a chance to ask him if, with enough prayer, healing could always be fully effected. He said he didn't know. He wished there could be extensive experimentation with the full cooperation of the medical profession. But so far there has not been. We still depend on anecdotal information, and there are enough quacks in this field to keep scientifically-minded people suspicious. Based on his impressions, however, he suggested that the responsiveness to prayer varies according to the problem. To take an extreme case, after a person has been dead for some time, Mr. Firestone would not expect any amount of prayer to bring the body back to life. That might mean also that a certain organ might decay to a point beyond recall even when the body as a whole was alive. Prayer seems most effective when it works with the life already there, supporting and encouraging it. But we shouldn't put strict limits on what can be accomplished. In some animals, some organs can grow back after they have been lost. Maybe with sufficient support, something like that can happen to a human body even when biologists don't expect it.

"To me, that seemed to fit our experience with Jennifer. The doctors say that certain parts of her brain were destroyed in the accident. They won't recover no matter how much we pray for her. Some of what she once was can't come back. But it also made me think that we shouldn't accept any limits on how much she can grow now with the other parts of her brain. They need all the encouragement we can give them, especially because her attitude is not very good. Maybe if we know better what we are praying for, we can help her more. Anyway, I'm not going to give up."

Sharon nodded enthusiastically. "I told you Janice was a great reporter. I bet she made it clearer than Mr. Firestone did!"

Dr. Robinson was no less impressed. He knew that as far as intelligence is concerned, we are never sharper than at eighteen, but he had never seen it demonstrated so clearly. "Sharon is right. You've done a really fine job for us. I've certainly got my money's worth. But what Fire-

stone says gives me a new problem. I've felt that
we cannot pray against people or even things. I
think I talked about that. Firestone encourages
people to experiment with cursing plants. I realize that in the New Testament we have the story
of Jesus cursing the fig tree, and I've never
known quite what to make of that. But on the
whole I've felt that is no model for us. Isn't there
a danger that prayer could be used as a weapon
against one's opponents? I even think of voodoo
dolls and all that. It makes me very uncomfortable."

"That kind of thing came up," Janice answered, "but I wish you had been there to push
it. Mr. Firestone's answer was that prayer is a
very powerful force, and it is important that we
use it only for good. He seems to think of his
role as making us aware of how we are interconnected and how important our prayers for others can be. Maybe he thinks that it is up to the
churches to get us to channel the power in the
right direction."

"It is frightening," David said, "to think that
our thoughts and feelings have effects beyond
our own bodies. So many of the effects could be
harmful. But I guess it is not too different from
anything else. We know we have the power to
help and to hurt by what we say and how we say
it. We know that it is important to say the right
things in the right ways. I guess we'll need to
learn that even unexpressed feelings can affect
others. It won't be as easy to suppose that we

have the right to think and feel as we please on the grounds that we are the only ones to suffer."

Mrs. Johnson was disturbed. "It sounds to me as though we now have a way of thinking of intercessory prayer that isn't prayer at all. When I pray, I address myself to God. But what Mr. Firestone is talking about doesn't seem to involve God at all. It's just another way that people influence one another. There's nothing wrong with that. I certainly believe we are related to one another in all sorts of ways. I've even had a habit of talking to my plants when I care for them, and people say I have a green thumb. But that's not prayer. It sounds as though the power of blessing and cursing comes from us, not from God!"

"That would mean," Bill said, "that we could just as well have addressed Jennifer's body as God. In fact, that might have been more honest! Instead of saying, 'Dear God, don't let Jennifer die!' we could have said, 'Jennifer, don't die!' At the time that would have been more comfortable for me, although I wouldn't have expected it to help. But now I don't like it. It felt like we were asking something, not commanding Jennifer to do something."

"Did anybody ask Mr. Firestone about that?" David asked Janice.

"Well, the question did come up in various ways," Janice answered. "But frankly, I don't think Mr. Firestone was comfortable with it. He certainly encouraged people to continue to pray to God. But when one woman said she practices meditation instead of prayer, he said that didn't matter, she could be just as effective. Sometimes he talked about prayer and meditation together as if there wasn't much difference. When someone asked him how he thought of God, he said that for him God was the Whole, that everything was connected with everything else in God—or something like that."

"I'm not sure I would go along with Mr. Firestone on his doctrine of God," said Dr. Robinson. "And I already said I don't like the way he talks about 'prayer.' But I do like what he says about the way things in the world are related. Even though God limits himself in order to allow us freedom, there's no doubt that he lets us have a great effect on one another. No one questions this when we talk about how we bring up children or organize society. Now we can add that how we think, feel, and pray affects other people, too, in ways that don't fit the older, scientific world view. I think that's an idea we can get used to. To think that way makes even more important the effect of prayer on what we say and how we feel about other people. Maybe the great importance of intercessory prayer is that it changes our destructive attitudes toward other people into positive ones."

"But once again, Dr. Robinson," Bill objected, "you make it sound as though the point of prayer was to change negative attitudes into positive ones. I cared a lot for Jennifer before I prayed for her. Maybe I care even more now. I don't know. But that's not what the prayer was about. It still sounds as though it wouldn't make much difference in our case whether we talked to God or to the cells in Jennifer's body!"

Dr. Robinson was a little hurt. He saw that Bill was right, but he felt that a more sympathetic interpretation of what he said was possible. He could feel himself becoming defensive, and he didn't want that. He thought he had finally established some rapport with a really extraordinary group of young people, and he didn't want to lose that. Better to admit that he didn't have the answers than to push onto them the answer he was fumbling for. "I'm sure there is a difference, Bill," he said at last. "And I'm surer than ever that your prayers had a lot to do with Jennifer's recovery. I hope you keep praying. I don't know what it will do for Jennifer, but I'm sure God will use it to support and strengthen her. She needs that help as much as ever. Maybe more.

"But as you spoke I remembered a church newsletter of a neighboring pastor. Ms. Williams has been writing quite a lot about prayer. I haven't paid much attention—I get so many newsletters—but it does seem to me that she may have thought about this matter more clearly than I have. I feel sure she would be glad to talk with us. Maybe I could ask her to join us next Sunday evening." The others nodded agreement. "And there's one more thing. Last time we met and talked about prayer, but we didn't pray. Could I pray with you today?" Again they nodded but continued to look to him for leadership. "No, I want to pray with you in your way," he said. "Please pray for Jennifer, and let me join in."

5 · MS. WILLIAMS

ONLY Dr. Robinson's years of dealing with all types of people enabled him to conceal his initial surprise and dismay as he opened the front door. *So young! he groaned silently. And I wonder what happened to her that her legs are so misshapen? She looks more like somebody's daughter I'd visit in the hospital after some awful accident than a colleague. And I'm turning to her for theological enlightenment?* Then he recognized his own pride and chauvinism and relaxed. He held out his hand and opened his heart to the Reverend Laura Williams.

"I really appreciate this chance to get to know you," Ms. Williams confessed when they were seated. "I'm new this year, you know, and I'm trying to meet my colleagues as quickly as I can. Actually, I feel pretty green. The truth is that I haven't finished my work at the seminary. I'm still writing a thesis."

Dr. Robinson relaxed even more. "I was a bit startled to see how young you looked," he admitted, "but seminary graduates are looking younger to me all the time. Tell me about your thesis. Could it be that you're writing about prayer and are trying out your ideas in the church newsletter?"

Ms. Williams laughed. "Guilty on both counts! You still know what it's like, don't you?"

"Are you familiar with the work of Mr. Firestone?" Dr. Robinson asked. "One of the girls coming this evening attended his Saturday workshop recently and gave us a fascinating résumé last week."

"I took the full workshop a couple of years ago," Ms. Williams replied. "I already knew I wanted to write about prayer, but that workshop really influenced the way I dealt with it."

"I'm beginning to think that providence had something to do with my thinking of your newsletters just when I did," said Dr. Robinson, "but here come the others. We won't need to spend much time in warm up, since you are already familiar with Firestone's ideas."

When they had all been introduced and had settled down again, Dr. Robinson told the group that Ms. Williams was familiar with Firestone and asked her to tell them something about herself and how she became interested in prayer.

"The answer to that goes back to childhood. I was one of the last victims of polio. Thank God for the vaccine and for what it has done to prevent cases in recent years! I was badly crippled. I grew up in a Christian home and in a rather conservative, pious church. I'm grateful for that. Of course I got all the medical treatment that I could, but in addition lots of people prayed for me and I was taught to pray for myself. I have no idea how much of my improvement to attribute to what, but the doctors have often expressed surprise at the extent of my recovery. And I have never doubted that I owed a great deal to prayer. So I can't remember when prayer was not important to me.

"My parents always taught me that I should not pray just for myself. There were other people, they often said, who did not have the blessings I had. I should pray for them, too. They were right. In spite of that, I think that I was rather too preoccupied with myself and my problems. I felt sorry for myself because I couldn't share in the activities of my peers. It was not until I was in seminary that I had any real dates. Maybe I still feel sorry for myself. But thanking God every day for the health she has given me and praying for others has helped to check that."

Sharon was fascinated by Ms. Williams and everything she said, but what startled her most was that Ms. Williams referred to God as "she." Sharon had to check that out. "Did you really speak of God as *she*?" she blurted out.

Ms. Williams was not surprised that that one point had overshadowed the rest. "Yes, I did. I usually do, but certainly not always. Of course, I don't believe that God is a woman, but I also have come to realize that God is not a man either. When we constantly say 'Father' and

'Lord' and 'he,' we inevitably think of God as a male even though we deny it verbally. No one believes God is an old man with a beard, but that is still the way our artists have drawn God. So it seems to me that it is important to use language and images that can break people of that habit of mind—even if they're shocking at first. Actually I don't see how any change can take place without some shock."

Without thinking what they were doing, the others all looked at Dr. Robinson. They wanted to know how he reacted to the idea that God was as much female as male. He was not pleased with the direction the conversation had taken. He would have preferred not to discuss Ms. Williams's language. If she liked to play that game, he had no objection. He just didn't want to make a big issue of it.

"I've tried in recent years to avoid using the masculine for the generic. I say 'he or she,' when that's what I mean. And I say 'human beings' instead of 'man' or 'mankind.' With respect to God I've been trying to introduce more feminine imagery into my prayers and sermons. I don't think it has bothered anyone. Perhaps no one has noticed. Ms. Williams is right that our language has been one-sided. It needs to become more balanced. But I've hoped that could happen gradually without shocking people. It would be better to evolve into balanced language over a hundred years than to tear the church apart now. I'm not happy about all the controversy over the inclusive lectionary. It will just set us back. Surely language is not that important!"

"Oh, but it is," Ms. Williams insisted. "I mean I used to think just as you do. But the more I studied feminist theologians and psychologists, the more I became convinced that it's very important. Just think of prayer, since that's what we came here to talk about. How we pray is very much affected by our idea or image of the One we're praying to. The image of 'heavenly Father' is very closely related to the old sky gods. It suggests that 'up above' somewhere there is One like an earthly father, only much more power-ful, who is taking care of things the way an earthly father does, only much better."

Sharon was intrigued but not ready to go along. "But I like thinking of God as a heavenly Father," she interjected. "I would have real trou-ble with a heavenly Mother. I just don't get along with Mom too well these days. She's cranky and inconsistent and downright unrea-sonable. Dad is steadier. I can always rely on him for love and good advice."

"Your point is well taken, Sharon," Ms. Williams laughed. "And we all have such differ-ent experiences with our own parents that it's risky to make any generalizations about God. But there does seem to be some kind of arche-type involved. In our early days, at least for most of us, the father is not always with us, but comes in from time to time. He lays down rules and enforces them. We're fascinated by his independence and power and we try to earn his approval by our obedience. Of course we feel some anger toward the father, too, because we are neither independent nor powerful, but that's another story.

"Now mother, at least as an archetype, is quite different. In our very early days she is always there, and the relationship is very intimate. We come from our mother and continue to receive our nurture from our mother's breasts. I don't want to beat this thing to death, but I think God is as much like a mother as a father. She gives us life and we continue to receive our lives moment by moment. I think God is with us always and her love is like a mother's unending tenderness."

Janice was thinking that, interesting as this was, it was time to get back to prayer. "I'm sure we could argue that point for days, Ms. Williams. But you said that how we think of God affects how we pray. Can you explain that to us? I think Dr. Robinson has told you that we are especially interested in intercessory prayer."

"It seems to me, Janice, that how we think about God affects what we expect our prayers to accomplish. If we pray to a kind of sky god, we are trying to influence some distant and maybe absent being to pay attention to us and act on our behalf. If, instead, we think of God as already here, God isn't above or outside watching what's going on but inside already taking part. We don't pray then to get God's attention, but rather to align ourselves with a presence that is already here. We reach out to others with and through a presence that is already working. We aren't pleading with God to do something that God would otherwise be reluctant to do." Ms. Williams paused for a moment.

David was getting excited. "This is really beginning to make some sense!" he exclaimed. "But you're going much too fast. Let me sort out the question as Bill put it last time and let's see how this fits.

"Bill made us all realize that if Mr. Firestone is right, then we can understand how our praying could have helped Jennifer. We could also understand why she improved rapidly for awhile and then stopped—or almost stopped. But the explanation doesn't say anything about God. It seems to turn out that the prayer part isn't important. We can meditate just as well or even command Jennifer's body to get well. It seems that intercessory prayer is another form of voodoo. We might use it for evil as well as good. Now the way you talk seems to bring God back into it, but I'm not sure how."

"Good. I'll try again, and take it one step at a time." Ms. Williams remembered how long it had taken her to come to her present understanding. It seemed so natural now to think that way that she too easily forgot the difficulties. "David, I was telling Dr. Robinson before you came in that I took Mr. Firestone's workshop a couple of years ago and found it helpful. I think I agree with almost everything he says. But I'm not satisfied with the way he passes over the difference between prayer and meditation. I think that *whether* we think of God and *how* are important. I've said that several times, haven't I? Anyway, I accept Mr. Firestone's idea of an interrelated world, and I connect it with the idea that God is interrelated with the world, too."

"That sounds great," David replied, "but confusing. God seems to be all mixed up with everything else. Does that really help us understand prayer?"

"I think so," Ms. Williams continued. "If when we pray we think of a God up there in heaven whom we need to persuade to intervene on earth, and then we discover that we can affect others directly by thinking of them, it will be very easy to interpret everything that happens without talking about God at all. There's no reason to think that first we influence God in heaven and then God decides to intervene on earth. The actual effects are much more easily understood as direct. Also, the idea of God sometimes being persuaded to intervene raises all sorts of problems. I'm sure you've thought of them. If it is good to intervene, why does God wait for someone to pray for it? If it is not good to intervene, why would God let someone's prayers influence him? (You see, I do say 'him' sometimes when I'm talking about that way of thinking of God.)"

"Yes," David said. "Why would God heal Jennifer halfway and then quit?"

"That's just the kind of question that makes me reject that whole way of thinking," Ms. Williams continued. "It doesn't work for me, and I don't think it works for anyone else either. It doesn't fit the evidence for the efficacy of intercessory prayers, among other things.

"Let's think of God not as way up there but as already here, everywhere. Think of a blade of grass. Above all, it is alive, and that's the mystery of it. God is in that life. A lot of people only want to see God in the big things, but I think of life itself as God. Now if one has the older world view, that doesn't make sense. In that view everything about the blade of grass can be explained in scientific terms—chemical composition, physical molecules, and so on. If that's not enough, then something supernatural, a life-force, say, has to be added to the picture. But if we can see that blade of grass relationally, we can see that much about it derives from its relations to the soil, the light, the moisture. I think its aliveness derives from its relation to God. The Bible supports the close association of God and life, and I think that for those who really accept the relational world view, there's lots of support in the study of living things. Of course, scientists are not likely to talk this way, especially as long as the word *God* means for them, as for so many others, the old sky god who intervenes from time to time with rain or thunderbolt."

"I hadn't realized it," Bill interjected, "but I guess I've thought of God that way—when I've thought of God at all. Maybe that's the reason I haven't seen much place for God in my life."

Ms. Williams continued, "Well, if I'm right, then God is always giving us life and trying to make us more alive. I don't mean only biological life; God makes us alive emotionally and intellectually, too. And I want to talk about the new birth and the new life as well. When we give thanks each day for what God is doing in us and for us, we give thanks for our life, our health, and our growth. We have in mind both our bodies and our psyches."

Mrs. Johnson was puzzled. "It's all very well to talk about God as life, Ms. Williams, but isn't that just one metaphor among others in the scriptures? I guess I've always emphasized another one: 'God is love.' How do we decide which language to use?"

"I wish I knew the answer to that one! I certainly don't want to insist that 'life' is the only way of thinking of God's presence. But I do find it a good one. Of course 'love' is a good one, too. So is 'truth'! All I really want to say is that it's biblical and helpful today to locate God's presence and work in life, wherever that is to be found. Emphasizing God's presence in all the life of the world helps to establish the contrast with the sky god imagery."

Sharon had been very quiet. But now she said, "I'm getting some idea of a different way to think about God and how God is with us, but I'm still puzzled about how that affects prayer. You're not going to be praying a heavenly Superman to get into action. But what *will* you do?"

"Well, Sharon," Ms. Williams answered, "I'm just beginning to develop a prayer style that fits the ideas I'm talking about. Maybe when I've finished my thesis, I'll have all the answers! No, seriously, I think you kids must pray better than I do. I've never had the dramatic results you have had. Still, your question deserves an answer, and I *am* sure that how we think about God affects how we pray. For one thing it keeps me from confusing prayer with cursing plants! But enough of that.

"When I pray, I don't primarily use words. I try to be attentive to the life within me and to get in harmony with it, to let it carry me beyond myself. Paul talked about how we don't know how to pray as we should and about how it is God's Spirit who prays through us (Rom. 8:26). That is the Spirit that, according to Paul, makes us alive. We could talk all along of the Spirit instead of life if we wanted. According to the creed, the Spirit is the Lord of life. I'm not happy with the lordship language, but I'll let that pass. Does this make sense so far?"

David wasn't sure that he really understood, but he liked what he heard all the same. "As I try to relate what you're saying to what we've experienced in our prayers, it seems to fit. We felt tremendously alive as we prayed. I think that's half the reason that we've kept it up, even though consciously it has been because of Jennifer. And that feeling of being very much alive also felt like the experience of God's being with us. I think the reason we resist saying that the praying to God wasn't necessary was that we felt that God was there. I still don't quite know what you mean by saying that God is life, but I'm willing to accept the idea for now. Maybe I'll even start studying what the Bible says about it!"

Ms. Williams smiled. "Good. I'm delighted that what I've said makes some sense to you so far. Lots of people just shut me off. If I criticize their images of God as way up there looking down on us, they feel that I've rejected God, whereas I feel that I've found her. OK? Will you let me say it that way again? You can say 'him' if that feels better to you.

"Now the next step is to recognize the validity of what Firestone and many other people teach—all living things are bound together in all sorts of ways. Did he give you some good examples, Janice?"

"Yes, indeed," Janice replied. "He told us about experiments in which galvanometers were attached to plant leaves. The readings would jump when brine shrimp were killed nearby. Some of the experiments are unbelievable! He said that we need to think of a whole field of living cells in which what happens to any of them affects all of them. We need to think of ourselves as part of that field."

"I think he has a good way of putting it," Ms. Williams said. "And I'm also convinced that in every one of those cells, God is at work. As a psychophysical organism I can hinder or even thwart that work in all sorts of ways. We all know that we can fail to exercise our bodies, eat too much sugar, sleep too little, and so forth. I think we now know also that we can, in biblical terms, choose death instead of life in our beliefs and attitudes. The effect on our cells is just as destructive, maybe more so, as when we inject the wrong chemicals into our bodies. But we can also choose life. That means that we'll be attentive to what our bodies are telling us. Most of all we'll be attentive to the Spirit that is the life of our souls. We'll trust it. (You notice that this time I'm trying out the neuter!) We'll let it carry us instead of trying to make it go where we want to go. In other words, we'll let it make us more alive. And when we do that, it supports life in all the cells in our bodies."

Bill broke in, "And are you saying that our attitudes, feelings, and beliefs have an effect on cells outside our bodies, too?"

Ms. Williams nodded. "Yes, I'm convinced that they do. But when the effect is general, it is also trivial. So here is where intercessory prayer comes in. When we align ourselves with the Spirit within us and are led by that Spirit to direct our prayers to the healing of another person, that general effect on all the cells in the world becomes focused on that other person. I admit I don't understand just how that happens. But there's evidence that it does happen.

"The result is not to persuade God to do what God otherwise is not willing to do. The result is to work with God in the healing of that other person. God is already at work, but the conditions are hostile. Perhaps the other person is choosing death. Our choice of life can make a difference. Or perhaps the other person is in a coma. That was the way with Jennifer, at first, wasn't it? I think your choice of life played the role that she could not play herself in her healing."

Bill was pleased. "So that means it really is God who heals and not our prayers, as Mr. Firestone's theories seem to imply. That feels much better. We helped make God's healing possible. Thanks, I like that way of thinking about it."

Mrs. Johnson was pleased, too. "What you are saying seems to fit with the idea of our being co-workers with God. I like to think of doctors as being co-workers with God when they provide chemicals that help make us well or when they set a bone in a broken arm. They don't do the healing. The best of them know that. Something wonderful is going on in the human body. The doctors remove obstacles and open up channels for God's more effective working. I like the idea that intercessory prayer works in a similar way. Yes, I think we are co-workers with God when we pray for the healing of another person."

"I'm so glad this makes sense to you," Ms. Williams responded. "I like to emphasize that God is working in the co-workers as well. God is not working only in the sick person but also in the doctors and the ones who are praying. It is not as if co-workers added some creaturely help to God. All of God's working is in and through creatures. God is working in and through the cells in all of our bodies and in and through our souls, too. God works whether or not we pay attention to it. But God's work seems to be most effective when we are aware of it, grateful for it, and align ourselves with it. And God works to make us aware, grateful, and aligned."

Dr. Robinson was uncomfortable. This was quite different from the way he usually thought about God. But he didn't want to get into an argument. He really wanted to be open, as long as the Christian faith was not threatened. There was certainly something to these new ideas if they weren't carried too far. But this was enough for one evening. "Thank you very much for coming this evening and for sharing so many fresh ideas with us. You make a lot of sense out of intercessory prayer, at least out of prayers for healing, but in the process you suggest ways of thinking of God that don't seem adequate to me. Maybe we can meet again to talk about that."

"That would be great for me," Ms. Williams replied. "I know I've talked too much, but I do want to thank all of you for letting me do it.

Hearing your questions and your responses has helped me to think more clearly about what I want to say in my thesis.

"Speaking of my thesis, my thesis advisor from the seminary will be coming to town next Sunday to preach at St. Mark's, and he's promised to come by to see me. I'll have a chance to talk to him about some of the issues that were raised here this evening."

"Is that James Hartwell?" Dr. Robinson asked. When Ms. Williams nodded, he continued, "Would there be any chance of getting him to join us for another conversation? I heard him speak once, and I was quite impressed. It would help me to know how he thinks about God in relation to the issues you have raised."

Sharon spoke for all the others when she enthusiastically seconded the suggestion. They agreed that they would meet next Sunday evening in any case, but they all hoped that Ms. Williams would persuade Professor Hartwell to join them. Before breaking up, they asked Ms. Williams to lead them in prayer.

She asked them to be silent for awhile, trying to be attentive to what was going on in their bodies, willing health and sensitivity. Then she asked the Spirit who gave life to all to heighten the life in Jennifer. They left quietly.

6 · PROFESSOR HARTWELL

PROFESSOR HARTWELL and Ms. Williams arrived a few minutes after the others had assembled. Professor Hartwell did not wait for Ms. Williams to introduce him.

"I'm James Hartwell," he said as the group rose to meet him. "Laura has been telling me about you. She says that last Sunday night she had such a good time pouring out her ideas that she's afraid she was too long-winded and professorial. It's clear that we professors have a bad name!"

"She had some exciting things to say that were quite new for us, Professor Hartwell," Mrs. Johnson replied. "By the way, I'm Edith Johnson. The young people met with me for supper this evening to go over some of the new ideas and prepare for our chance to talk with you. We surely do appreciate your coming."

Sharon spoke first. "I was bothered last week by Ms. Williams's insistence on talking about God as a woman. I've kept thinking about that all week. Sometimes it seems OK. But it's still so strange. Do you talk about God that way, too, professor?"

"No, I don't. Let's see, are you Janice or Sharon?"

"I'm Sharon. That's Janice. The others are David, Bill, and Dr. Robinson."

"Thanks, I didn't give anyone a chance for introductions. Sorry. But as to your question, Sharon, I try to avoid speaking of God as either male or female. Of course, deeply entrenched habits and the dominant language of scripture make it hard to avoid talking of 'Lord' and 'Father.' So I'm glad there are some, like Laura, who use feminine language. It grates on me, but it keeps making me think."

Dr. Robinson was determined not to get stuck on that issue again. "I'm more bothered about something else. Traditionally the Christian understanding of God has emphasized the personal nature of that God. If God is thought of just as life, that personal nature is lost. God becomes a general principle or force."

"Oh, but I didn't mean that." Ms. Williams interrupted him. "God seems very personal to me. I guess I just didn't make that clear. I talked mostly about God's presence as the life within us. I didn't talk about how God has her own life as well. But Dr. Hartwell can say it better. Most of my ideas I've learned from him."

"Thanks, Laura, I'm proud to claim credit for your thinking, even if I don't deserve much of it. Your way of putting things, in terms of 'life,' for example, is your own. But the concepts that underlie your language I share with you. I think of God as Cosmic Person or Spirit and, of course, as very much alive. And, like you, I think of God as present in every creature. And, yes, it is this presence that gives life to those that are alive. Chapter 1 of John's Gospel speaks of the Word that enlivens the creatures. I think of that as a very important part of what God is doing. John's Gospel also talks about the light that enlightens all human beings, and I like that imagery, too. But I guess you could think of that light as a fuller expression of life, the life of the mind, for example."

"Well, that relieves much of my concern," Dr. Robinson responded. "I've grown suspicious of some recent theological writings. So often God seems to be nothing more than a principle or human idea of some kind. But a cosmic Person who gives life and light to the world through his presence in the world, and especially in us— that sounds like the God of the Bible. Is that what you were saying, Ms. Williams?"

"Yes, I suppose so . . . but I'd have to add one thing that I think I learned from Professor Hartwell, even if the emphasis is my own. As Mr. Firestone taught me, all things are relational, and living things especially are richly interconnected. Human life is relational at an even more sophisticated or complex level, and I believe God is what I would call 'perfectly' relational. Christians have always maintained that God is omniscient—that he knows everything that is going on at all times. But 'knowing' in the Bible means something much more immediate and intimate than just having information. I think

God shares our experiences with us and with all things everywhere. She experiences our joy and suffering as we experience it and that affects the way God works for life now and tomorrow— with us and with everything that is."

"That's a different way of putting it," Mrs. Johnson commented. "But I think I've always believed something like that. Surely God is with us in both joy and sorrow. I felt that especially when Sue died. She was my daughter, and she lived only two months. It was awful. But I felt God with me, and I seemed to be able to share my suffering with him."

"I can't object to that either," Dr. Robinson said. "But isn't there a danger of putting a one-sided emphasis on God's immanence? When you made fun of the sky god image, Ms. Williams, I felt you weren't fair to the idea of God as transcendent. Maybe transcendence is a masculine image. I don't know. But it is certainly important to me and to most Christians. I don't object to supplementing images of transcendence with those of immanence. And in the long run I think we do need to balance masculine images with feminine ones, too. But when you talked, it didn't sound like balancing. It sounded as though you were replacing one set with the other. I'll have to admit I found it offensive!"

"Laura probably does overstate her case some-times," Professor Hartwell interceded, "at least from my point of view. But I don't think that

transcendence is any more personal than immanence. One could argue the reverse. For me,
incarnation is the central Christian doctrine.
That implies that what is transcendent is immanent and what is immanent is transcendent."

"I hate to interrupt," said Mrs. Johnson, "but
all these words! You two are enjoying this, I can
see, but I wonder if the questions of these four
young people are being answered."

"Well, I'm trying to follow," Bill offered, "but
it seems a bit like a tempest in a teapot. If there's
a God, he goes beyond us (I think that's what
transcendence means). And Professor Hartwell
is saying that the incarnation means that that
same God is with us in the here and now—Ms.
Williams would say she is intimately with us—
bodily and emotionally. I just don't see any big
problem. If it's really true, it's pretty wonderful."

"You're right, Bill," Dr. Robinson acknowl-
edged, somewhat sheepishly. "How often I've
seen church leaders denouncing one another
when the issue is simply one of images and
emphasis, not truth and error. So much of our
disagreement is the result of personal dif-
ferences. I admit I am cautious by nature, and I
am reluctant to shock people because I fear they
will simply run away or shut me off. Maybe it
helps when somebody less fearful stirs things
up.

"But indulge me for a moment. I have one
other question. It's such a relief to be in a group
where I can ask questions—and not be expected

to have all the answers. It's about divine power. The way Ms. Williams talks, I get the impression that God doesn't really have much power of his own. I agree that God isn't making everything happen just as he likes. That makes nonsense of sin. I'm sure God limits himself so that we can have scope for our freedom. But I also feel sure that God remains omnipotent and that God could force us to do his will if he wanted to. It's just that God wants our free obedience, not mere outward conformity."

Professor Hartwell thought a moment. "There does seem to be a real difference between you and Laura on this point, Dr. Robinson. That may be connected with her feminism and your masculine point of view. But the same issue can be found throughout the scriptures."

"To me, Dr. Robinson," Ms. Williams broke in, "you sound as though you think of power as the ability to control outward behavior. I think that is the kind of power that goes with the older scientific world view. It rearranges the atoms and alters their motion. So God could snatch a car out of the way of a speeding train at a railroad crossing if he wanted to. He just doesn't, because he doesn't want to interfere with human freedom.

"I've come to think of power differently. If we accept the relational vision, then we need a relational understanding of power. The power to empathize with others seems to me an important form of power—also the power to give other people new ideas and images, new ways of organizing their world. The power to make alive and to extend the scope of human love is a tremendously important form of power. I think of God's power along these lines."

Dr. Robinson didn't want to be simply categorized as an adherent of the older scientific world view. He appreciated what he had learned of the relational way of thinking, and he wanted to incorporate it. "Touché! The way I stated my ideas deserved that answer. I'm trying to learn to think more relationally, and I like what you say about relational power. But if we take the image of an earthly father—no, let's say 'parent' to avoid that issue—you are certainly right that the power exercised is mostly of the kind you're talking about. I've frequently preached along those lines. And I've pointed out how an earthly parent needs to let the child make a mistake and learn from that experience as well as to teach and give examples. I've also talked about how God is with us in our suffering, not as the One who makes us suffer, but as the One who suffers with us. So we're not so far apart after all.

"But the earthly parent *can* snatch the child out of the way of the car. That kind of power belongs to parents, too! The fact that parents refrain from exercising it all the time does not mean that it doesn't exist or should never be used. Why should we think that God lacks that power?"

"That's a tough one," admitted Ms. Williams.

"I guess I'm not always fair when I criticize positions I don't like and you've really been a gentleman in response. You put me on the spot. I just don't have a good answer for that one."

"That is a good exchange," Professor Hartwell said enthusiastically. "I confess I think it's good for Laura to be made to realize how she sometimes sounds. It has not been easy being her advisor! She's so bright and confident! She's almost too smart for her own good." He grinned at her. It was obvious they liked each other and were on relaxed terms. "But even so, I'll accept some responsibility for her basic point.

"For years I tried to think of God as having a great deal of power that God chose not to exercise—along the lines you suggest, Dr. Robinson. But in the end, I gave that up. It made the problem of evil insoluble for me. If God could have stopped the Holocaust but chose not to do so to avoid interfering with the freedom of a few Nazis, I can hardly forgive God. Even now, if God could restore Jennifer to perfect health, I cannot understand why God holds back. Why would God bring her back this far and then stop midway? The idea of God's leaving space for human freedom doesn't go very far toward explaining this, does it?

"The final decision came for me as I thought about the threat of a nuclear holocaust that might put an end to human life altogether. What do I really think God will do if we punch the buttons that start the missiles on the way?

Will God let us destroy ourselves for the sake of respecting our freedom? What would be the point? But if not, how would God intervene? I'm just trying to be completely honest with you and with myself. I don't expect God to act in a fundamentally different way then from the way God acts now. And that means to me that I don't seriously believe God is holding all that power in reserve. What do you think, Dr. Robinson? If your own child were threatened by a snake or a falling boulder, you would certainly intervene. Do you think the omnipotent Parent will snatch the missiles out of the sky?"

"Well, you certainly know how to go to the heart of the matter, professor," Dr. Robinson said after a moment. "You've gone right to the question that I've found hardest to deal with. I can understand God's holding back in ordinary circumstances—yes, even in the Holocaust—but it doesn't seem to make sense that he would let the whole world of living creatures be destroyed. Yet when I ask myself how God would intervene, I keep thinking of the way he calls us now to work against war. It is as hard for me to picture God's stopping the missiles in midair as it is for you. Surely he could. Yet I guess I don't really expect him to do it. But I can't think of any reason for God to hold back at that time."

Sharon had been listening to this exchange very carefully. "I don't know if I told you," she ventured cautiously, "but I grew up in a very

conservative church. We stopped going years
ago, but I vividly remember what I was taught in
Sunday school. My teacher definitely believed
that the earth was going to be destroyed in a
final great war she called Armageddon. It would
last for years and annihilate everyone and everything, but in the middle of it Jesus would come
for all the Christians and keep them safe until
it was all over. Then God would make a new
heaven and earth for those Jesus was keeping
safe. And all the Christians who had died would
be resurrected and join them. But this would be
only for Christians, so it was very important to
be 'born again.' She said that repeatedly."

"I grew up in that tradition myself," Professor
Hartwell smiled, "but to me it just doesn't sat-
isfy. I can't believe that the God who didn't
rescue the Christian Armenians when the Turks
were slaughtering them or the God who let the
Jews be horribly experimented on and led to the
gas chambers will suddenly change now and
snatch us from the horrors of an all-out atomic
war. It just isn't consistent with what we know of
God through history and in Jesus Christ.

"If we do destroy our earth, I have no doubt
that, after great grieving, God will begin again
with radioactive dust and with the cockroaches
and scorpions the scientists predict may survive
and work with whatever else is available to
achieve whatever is possible under those circumstances. And I believe that the human experience would somehow be preserved in God (I'm

not saying *how* because I don't know), but the loss would be enormous.

"This is actually what drove me from my tradition and made me a seeker first and then a professor. When I thought of the grief and pain of an Armageddon—not just human grief but the pain of a whole earth dying—I just could not be a part of a tradition that could be so cheerful about the prospect of the whole world perishing in unspeakable anguish as long as they were saved. That sort of thinking seems totally opposed to everything I believe about God and about what it means to live in relationship to God in the world God has made and is making."

Mrs. Johnson spoke, "I keep thinking of Jesus dying on the cross—and of some of your sermons, Dr. Robinson. You've sometimes contrasted the power of Christ crucified with that of the Roman legions. It's a powerful contrast. I've been moved by it. We see God more in the cross than in the legions. I don't think you meant that the legions are a poor way of thinking of God's power just because God respects our freedom. Isn't it a question of what kind of power God exercises rather than how much?"

"That's a really profound point, Mrs. Johnson." Professor Hartwell was genuinely impressed. It had taken him years of struggle before he came to the same conclusion. "I agree with you. God's power is not like that of the legions or of Superman. God works creatively, persuasively, redemptively in every creature. That's the only way God works. God is the giver of life, not its destroyer. At least that's the conclusion I've reached.

"Paul Tillich kept telling us that God is not another being alongside the creatures. I'm not sure I agree with him on that. I think the Cosmic Person is another Person in addition to all of us human persons. But I also think that God is a very different kind of person. As youths we used to sing that God has no hands but our hands and no feet but our feet. I think that's true. God works in and through creatures, not like another more powerful creature alongside us. If we creatures refuse to do what God calls us to do, God's purposes won't be accomplished. That may be frightening. But I think it's true!"

"My head is spinning," Bill confessed to the group. "I'm just not ready for all of this. I've been trying to stay with it by relating it to the specifics of our praying for Jennifer. It seems to me that in general we need to do some thinking before we just launch into prayer. We need to be sure that what we're praying for is what God is working for. Maybe we need to be responsive to God's working in us before we ask him to work somewhere else. If Professor Hartwell is right, there's no point in asking God to intervene. That seems strange at first. Until recently I strongly suspected that there might not be any God at all; but if there were a God, I assumed he could do anything. It would just be a matter of persuading him to do it. (Sorry, Ms. Williams, I'm not ready to say 'she' and 'her' yet!) So now I'm wondering what all this God talk means in relation to how we pray for Jennifer. Maybe instead of praying for the old Jennifer to be restored to herself and to us, we should pray for the growth of the present Jennifer from where she now is. Maybe much more growth could take place if we would let go of the other hope and accept what is. Maybe she could grow to be a much happier and more capable young woman if she didn't feel from all of us the contrast between what she is now and what she was. Maybe I need to stop thinking of her as my girl friend, too."

Ms. Williams was delighted by his sensitivity. "I think you're exactly right. I hadn't thought of it just that way myself, but when you said it, I felt you had understood the implications of my ideas better than I had. There's only one place I would put it differently. All that work in getting clear what to pray for and being sure that the praying itself is with God is also prayer, or at least it can be."

Mrs. Johnson added, "This conversation has made me realize keenly that we do indeed need to be careful what we pray for. We all reacted negatively to the idea that cursing the plants was a form of prayer. But I've been in prayer groups that asked God to change particular people in particular ways, ways that those people did not want to be changed. Of course, those who were praying thought they knew best. But maybe they didn't. Maybe, if they had spent more time getting their own desires in line with God's, they wouldn't have worked so hard to get other people to change. I don't know."

"It is kind of scary, isn't it?" Janice burst in. She was almost in tears. "Maybe we shouldn't have prayed for Jennifer at all. Maybe it would have been better for her to die than to live as a misfit and be miserable all her life. I hate to think that, but if I'm honest, I would rather die than live like that."

Sharon didn't want to let Janice leave it there. "I don't believe that, Janice. That would mean that the doctors were wrong in trying to save her life, too. If we went to the extreme, we would almost have to have some revelation of God's will before we could do anything for anyone. It always might turn out to be wrong. I don't believe we can live that way. We have to try to help people, and if one way to help is by praying, we ought to pray for them. We ought not to find praying any more scary than going to visit them or giving them medicine."

Sharon's wisdom relieved the tension. Janice had voiced something that had been at the edge of the thoughts of several but had been unspoken.

"Thanks, Sharon." It was David's turn. "Janice said just what I had begun to think, and you freed me from that fear. It wasn't wrong for us to be co-workers with God in Jennifer's partial recovery. Now I feel a responsibility to stay with her, to become a friend to the new Jennifer. That way I think I can work with God, helping Jennifer to become more alive.

"I doubt that prayer is the main thing now, though I don't want to stop praying. Maybe we could get Jennifer involved in praying with us, and maybe that would really help her. But mainly I want to help her develop specific skills, like reading and writing, by practice and hard work. I don't think prayer will be a shortcut."

It was time to close. Janice turned to Dr. Robinson. "Will you lead us in prayer tonight?"

"Sure, Janice, but I must admit I'm more self-conscious about praying right now than I've been for a long time. Still, I've found that when I feel unsure, I need to take that to God, too. Let's pray!

"Dear God, you who are to us as both Father and Mother, thank you for these precious hours we have had together. Thank you for the persons gathered here, for the honesty of their questioning and the aliveness of their minds. Thank you for working through them to make me think more clearly about you and about prayer.

"We thank you also that you have shown yourself to us in Jesus as One who understands our confusion and our failures. Help us to be open to new ideas and to find you more clearly through them.

"We remember Jennifer before you, and the

awful tragedy that still is a tragedy, and we realize that life will always contain pain and disappointment. Yet we thank you for preserving her life and restoring her to us. Help us to love her now for what she is, and use our love—together with the prayers and the other actions that express it—to bring her to such health, happiness, and helpfulness as her capacities will allow.

"Continue to bless these young people, who have themselves been such a blessing, by making them aware of yourself and what they can become. May we all know your presence and guidance in joy and in sorrow. For we pray in Jesus' name. *Amen.*"

JOHN B. COBB, JR. is Professor of Theology at the School of Theology, Claremont, California. He received his Ph.D. degree from the Divinity School at the University of Chicago.

A member of the California-Pacific Conference of the United Methodist Church, Dr. Cobb has written many books in the areas of theology and prayer, including: *To Pray or Not to Pray, Talking about God, Process Theology as Political Theology, Theology and Pastoral Care,* and *Christ in a Pluralistic Age.*

Dr. Cobb and his wife Jean have four married sons and two grandchildren.